Lauren Child

I am not sleepy and I will not go to bed

Featuring

Charlie and Lola

A special thank you to Mrs Fish at Big Fish
and hello to Little Fish

Perry

For Perry with a
squilllion thanks for a
zillion favours

(p.s. i hope this typeface isn't a style crime)

For the supremely stylish,
and fantastically fabulous,

Sandro and Piera
with love from
Lauren

ORCHARD BOOKS
Carmelite House
50 Victoria Embankment
London EC4Y 0DZ
First published in 2001 by Orchard Books
This edition published in 2015

ISBN 978 1 84616 884 0
Text and illustrations © Lauren Child 2001 & 2015
The right of Lauren Child to be identified as the author and
illustrator of this work has been asserted by her in accordance with the
Copyright, Designs and Patents Act, 1988.
A CIP catalogue record for this book is available from the British Library.
4 6 8 10 9 7 5   Printed in China
Orchard Books An imprint of Hachette Children's Group
Part of The Watts Publishing Group Limited An Hachette UK Company
www.hachette.co.uk

I have this little sister Lola.
She is small and very funny.
Sometimes I have to keep an eye on her.
Sometimes Mum and Dad ask me to try and
get her off to bed.
This is a hard job
because Lola likes to stay up late.

Lola likes to stay up colouring

and

scribbling

and

sticking

and

wriggling

and

bouncing

and most of all

chattering.

Usually, when I say,
    "Lola, Mum says it is time for bed,"
        she says,
    "No! I am NOT sleepy and

                    I
                WILL
                NOT
            go to bed."
                I say,

                    "But all the birds
                        have gone to sleep."

She says,
"But I am **not** a bird,
Charlie."

"But you must be slightly sleepy, Lola,"
   I say.
      Lola says,
   "I am not slightly sleepy at 6

or 7

or 8

and I am still
   wide awake at 9

and not at all tired at 10

11

12

and I will probably still be perky at even **13** O'CLOCK in the morning."

Lola says she **never** gets tired.

One night I said,
"But if there's
no bedtime there
can be no
bedtime drink and it's
pink milk
tonight."
(Lola really likes
pink milk.)
"Are you sure
you don't want
to go to bed?"

"But Charlie," says Lola, "if I have pink milk,
the tigers will want pink milk too."
"Tigers," I say, "what tigers?"
                "The tigers at the table, Charlie,
they are waiting for their bedtime drink.
        Tigers get very cross if they have to wait."

So I make Lola and

three tigers pink milk.

Then I say,
"Let's go and brush our teeth."

So Lola says, "But Charlie, I can't brush my teeth
because somebody is eating my toothbrush."
"But who would eat your toothbrush?" I say.
Lola says, "I think it's that lion,
I saw him brushing his teeth with my toothbrush
and now he's gobbling it all up."
"But this looks like your brush, Lola," I say.
"Oh," says Lola,
"he must be using yours."

brush their teeth.

Then I say, "You have to have
a bath. You look a bit grubby."
"Who says?" says Lola.
"Mum does," I say. "She's coming
to check in ONE minute."
And then what do you think Lola says?
"But Charlie, I can't have a bath
because of the whales."
"What whales?
Where?"
I say,
looking
about.

"The whales who are swimming
in the bath, they're taking up all of
the room," she says.
"Well what do you want me
to do about it?" I ask.
"Maybe you will have to help me
shoo ONE of them down
the plug hole," says Lola.
So I help Lola shoo

one

  whale

    down

     the

      plug

       hole.

And

then

Lola

hops

into

the

bath.

"Now, Lola," I say. "Where are your pyjamas?"

"I don't have any pyjamas, Charlie," she says.

I say, "What about these ones under your pillow?"

"Those are not my pyjamas," says Lola, shaking her head.

"Oh no, those pyjamas belong to two dancing dogs."

"Well, do you think they would let you just borrow their pyjamas?" I ask.

"Maybe," says Lola.
"But you will
have to go
and telephone them."

"They say pyjamas suit you better than them.
You can wear them whenever you like." – – – – –

And so Lola
pops on
her pyjamas.

At last
Lola is ready for bed and I say,

"Now, Lola,
I have given three **tigers**
their bedtime drink

and

watched a **lion**
gobbling my toothbrush

and

shooed one
whale
down
the
plug
hole

and

telephoned two
dancing dogs
about pyjamas.

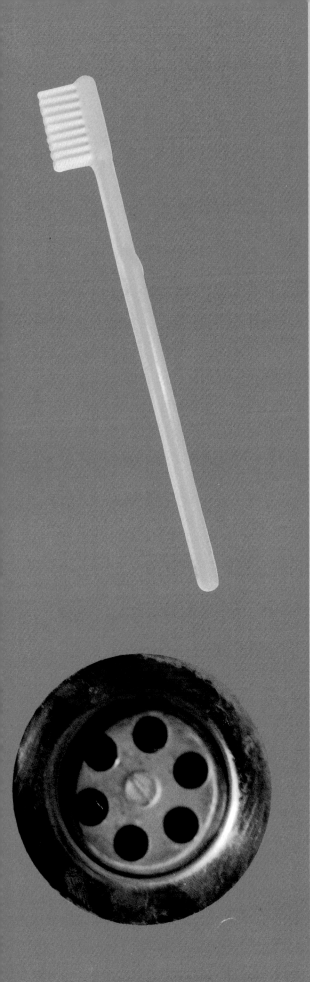

NOW

will

you

please

hop

into

bed."

Lola says,
"Yes, yes, Charlie,
I'm hopping,
I'm hopping..."

"But I think there's one in **yours**," says Lola,
as she climbs into bed.

"Goodnight Charlie.
Goodnight Hipp**i**pot**i**mus."